Written by Dana Meachen Rau
Illustrated by Jan Bryan-Hunt

Reading Advisers:

Gail Saunders-Smith, Ph.D., Reading Specialist

Dr. Linda D. Labbo, Department of Reading Education,
College of Education, The University of Georgia

LEVEL C

A COMPASS POINT
EARLY READER

For Mildred Jensen

A Note to Parents

As you share this book with your child, you are showing your new reader what reading looks like and sounds like. You can read to your child anywhere—in a special area in your home, at the library, on the bus, or in the car. Your child will associate reading with the pleasure of being with you.

This book will introduce your young reader to many of the basic concepts, skills, and vocabulary necessary for successful reading. Talk through the details in each picture before you read. Then read the book to your child. As you read, point to each word, stopping to talk about what the words mean and the pictures show. Your child will begin to link the sounds of the letters with the look of the words that you and he or she read.

After your child is familiar with the story, let him or her read the story alone. Be careful to let the young reader make mistakes and correct them on his or her own. Be sure to praise the young reader's abilities. And, above all, have fun.

Gail Saunders-Smith, Ph.D.
Reading Specialist

Consulting editor: Rebecca McEwen

Compass Point Books
3722 West 50th Street, #115
Minneapolis, MN 55410

Visit Compass Point Books on the Internet at *www.compasspointbooks.com* or e-mail your request to *custserv@compasspointbooks.com*

Library of Congress Cataloging-in-Publication Data
Rau, Dana Meachen.
   I'll make you a card / written by Dana Meachen Rau ; illustrated by Jan Bryan-Hunt.
      p. cm. — (Compass Point early reader)
   "Level C."
   Summary: Handmade cards are given to celebrate a holiday for each month of the year.
   ISBN 0-7565-0172-5 (hardcover)
   [1. Greeting cards—Fiction. 2. Holidays—Fiction. 3. Stories in rhyme.] I. Bryan-Hunt, Jan, ill. II. Title. III. Series.
   PZ8.3.R232 Il 2002
   [E]—dc21   2001004728

JANUARY						
S	M	T	W	Th	F	S
		1	2	3	4	5
6	7	8	9	10	11	12
13	14	15	16	17	18	19
20	21	22	23	24	25	26
27	28	29	30	31		

In January, I'll make you a card
to ring in the new year.

In February, I'll make you a card

because I love having you near.

In March, I'll make you a card

MARCH						
S	M	T	W	Th	F	S
					1	2
3	4	5	6	7	8	9
10	11	12	13	14	15	16
17	18	19	20	21	22	23
24/31	25	26	27	28	29	30

with a green crayon and pen.

In April, I'll make you a card

APRIL						
S	M	T	W	Th	F	S
	1	2	3	4	5	6
7	8	9	10	11	12	13
14	15	16	17	18	19	20
21	22	23	24	25	26	27
28	29	30				

Have a nice day!

because spring is here again.

In May, I'll make you a card

MAY						
S	M	T	W	Th	F	S
			1	2	3	4
5	6	7	8	9	10	11
12	13	14	15	16	17	18
19	20	21	22	23	24	25
26	27	28	29	30	31	

because you're my mom and I'm glad.

Best
Dad

In June, I'll make you a card

			JUNE			
S	M	T	W	Th	F	S
						1
2	3	4	5	6	7	8
9	10	11	12	13	14	15
16	17	18	19	20	21	22
23/30	24	25	26	27	28	29

because you sure are the best dad!

In July, I'll make you a card

JULY						
S	M	T	W	Th	F	S
	1	2	3	4	5	6
7	8	9	10	11	12	13
14	15	16	17	18	19	20
21	22	23	24	25	26	27
28	29	30	31			

painted red, white, and blue.

In August, I'll make you a card

AUGUST						
S	M	T	W	Th	F	S
				1	2	3
4	5	6	7	8	9	10
11	12	13	14	15	16	17
18	19	20	21	22	23	24
25	26	27	28	29	30	31

after a day at the beach with you!

In September, I'll make you a card

SEPTEMBER						
S	M	T	W	Th	F	S
1	2	3	4	5	6	7
8	9	10	11	12	13	14
15	16	17	18	19	20	21
22	23	24	25	26	27	28
29	30					

because fall is in the air.

In October, I'll make you a card

OCTOBER						
S	M	T	W	Th	F	S
		1	2	3	4	5
6	7	8	9	10	11	12
13	14	15	16	17	18	19
20	21	22	23	24	25	26
27	28	29	30	31		

that might give you quite a scare!

In November, I'll make you a card

NOVEMBER

S	M	T	W	Th	F	S
					1	2
3	4	5	6	7	8	9
10	11	12	13	14	15	16
17	18	19	20	21	22	23
24	25	26	27	28	29	30

to thank you for being you.

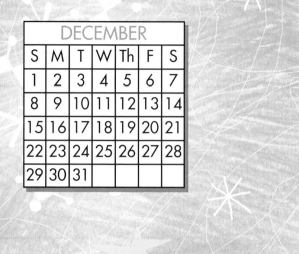

In December, I'll make you a card

with candles and snowflakes, too!

So when the year is done

and the cards are on the shelf,

we'll remember these happy months

with the cards I made myself.

More Fun with Cards!

Making cards together can be a fun opportunity for you and your child to explore your creative sides, share special time, and give something to others. And because there are so many holidays throughout the year, there are many occasions to make cards. Making cards is also a great way to teach about recycling by taking something used once and making it into something new.

Reserve an empty box or drawer in your home. Fill it with card-making supplies. They could be anything—scraps of colored paper, colorful pictures from magazines, wrapping paper and bows, family photos, old greeting cards, and even shiny gum wrappers or sandpaper. When a holiday or birthday comes along, dive into the box or drawer and choose fun items to make a special card together.

Word List

(In this book: 80 words)

a	green	painted
after	happy	pen
again	having	quite
air	here	red
and	I	remember
April	I'll	ring
are	I'm	scare
at	in	September
August	is	shelf
beach	January	snowflakes
because	July	so
being	June	spring
best	love	sure
blue	made	thank
candles	make	that
card	March	the
cards	May	these
crayon	might	to
dad	mom	too
day	months	we'll
December	my	when
done	myself	white
fall	near	with
February	new	year
for	November	you
give	October	you're
glad	on	

About the Author

Dana Rau loves to create things. She is the author of more than sixty books for children and has illustrated some as well. Ever since she was a little girl, she has made cards for holidays and birthdays. She has a drawer in her home in Farmington, Connecticut, filled with supplies. Once she makes a mess gluing everything together, she cleans up, puts her cards in envelopes, and gives them to her favorite people.

About the Illustrator

Jan Bryan-Hunt is a freelance artist who lives in Kansas City, Missouri, with her husband and two children. Some of her favorite things to do are painting furniture, making jewelry, and most of all, making "stuff" with her children, Bryan and Amy. Another family favorite is going to the park where they have spotted as many as fifty deer, a few foxes, and several turkeys.